Nest Egg

Nest Egg

BY
BARTOLOMEU CAMPOS QUEIROS

TRANSLATED BY
JANE SPRINGER

Drawings by Alina Gavrielatos

A Groundwood Book
Douglas & McIntyre
Vancouver/Toronto

Copyright © 1988 Bartolomeu Campos Queiros
Translation copyright © 1992 by Groundwood Books
Originally published in 1988 as *Indez* by Editora
Miguilim, Brazil.

Canadian Cataloguing in Publication Data

Queiros, Bartolomeu Campos
    Nest egg

Translation of: Indez.
ISBN 0-88899-159-2

I. Title.

PZ7.Q45Ne 1992   j869.3   C92-093470-6

Groundwood Books
Douglas & McIntyre Ltd.
585 Bloor Street West
Toronto, Ontario
M6G 1K5

Illustrations by Alina Gavrielatos
Design by Michael Solomon
Printed and bound in Canada

To Yeda Prates Bernis

CONTENTS

Nest Egg

Compliments
of the Morning

SPRING, summer, autumn and winter were names associated with other kingdoms. Here people knew only the rainy season and the dry season. This was a place where the year was divided into the sun and the rain, and was broken up by the "widow's wedding" — sun and rain at the same time — embellished by the rainbow.

During the rains, there were floods that had the cattle climbing up to the mountain top, fleeing their death. There were the lightning flashes of St. Peter's whip, which tore open the sky, and the dark clouds accompanied by thunder that frightened even the small ground animals. Small bits of perfumed soap would collect in the eaves of the roof as if making a wish: "Clara, make the sun come and dry our sheets." But the rains would just promise more rain.

With the dry season came dips in the river. It was the time of bonfires to honour the saints of June — St. Antonio, St. John, St. Peter. Then with the winds of August tearing off the clouds, people would tell stories, between drinks, of monsters dressed in clouds of cotton.

It was the time for walks in the woods with the heart praying:

St. Bento, holy water,
Jesus Christ of the altar.
Move away snake, move away insect,
let the son of God pass by.

And at the edge of night in the back yard the dancing circle spun full of ballads:

If this street were mine,
    circle around,
    melon chapel,
I would order them to put up tiles,
    stay and shake,
so that Father Francisco would enter
    the circle, circle around,
and I am poor, poor, poor, in the palm
    of my hand, circle around.

The children played pass the ring or blind man's bluff. Our parents, who were feeling lazy at that hour, read the future in the movement of the stars, the colour of the clouds, the size of the moon and the direction of the winds.

The world was not divided into two—one for grownups, the other for the little ones. Everyone shared the same emotions. All were made happy by the wedding feasts, the June dances, the baptismal lunches. Everyone experienced the same sadness during Lent and the same anguish when the dry season killed the crops.

And when the chickens began to get fat, it was a sign that a new baby was about to arrive. The child was greeted with the same joy with which the family ate the chicken wings, back, feet, neck and leftover soup smothered in celery and a smell that fortified the mother recuperating on her white bed.

On the day that the child's umbilical cord fell off, the midwife, godmother of all births, would bury it in a chosen place. If it was buried in the flower garden, the girl would be beautiful and a good gardener. If it was buried in the vegetable garden, the boy would be a farmer, or if in the corral, a cowboy. And so was destiny chosen.

In this way, being born was so beautiful that it was very easy to believe in another life.

Antonio arrived during the rainy season. They say he was born before his time. His family asked the neighbours for fattened chickens and dried his clothes on the side of the oven. They flung his umbilical cord into the stream. He was born so weak that he was baptized at home, quickly, without any celebration. For godparents they chose a couple of close friends, to whom they made many apologies for the haste. Death without baptism would have condemned the boy, innocent as he was, to live forever in limbo, a place without light.

Everyone wanted to see the boy — the premature fruit — wrapped in finely embroidered and colourful fringed eiderdowns, asleep in the corner of his mother's bed. But Antonio, as if still drowned in a world previous to our own, did not notice the visitors. He showed little sign of interest in the life around him. He let out a mumble, wrinkled his forehead, gave a slow stretch and closed his eyes to avoid the pain caused by the light of the outside.

Between fevers and colds, ointments and plasters, Antonio gradually began to be in the world, loved by his brother and sisters, friends of the family and the most distant relatives. Who could not appreciate a boy who was born unexpectedly, without respecting the calendar?

From the start, Antonio required a lot of work. You had to go long distances to fetch the strong milk of the retreating goats. You had to protect him from drafts and the cool night air, and bathe him in lukewarm mallow water, without forgetting teas of fennel, pennyroyal, anise and camomile.

When Antonio complained, Dona Luzia would come with a small branch of rue and bless him to protect him from the changing wind, from weakness and from the evil eye. All the saints that protect children were called in to give their support; and the prayers would go on for three, nine or thirteen days, in the neighbours' presence.

Antonio was neither homely nor handsome. Some said he had his father's face when he was young. Others saw his mother's nose and his grandfather's chin. And others said he looked like an angel — bless God! — except that he had no wings.

But what was different about him was the cow-lick high up on his forehead, close to his soft spot that made his few fine hairs stand on end. With his hair splayed out like that his eyes seemed larger. His face transformed into surprise in the sun, before it became used to the light.

Like all children, Antonio passed his time trying to taste his feet, looking at his hands in the air and, for a long time, biting the rungs of his cradle. His mother would roll up wood shavings in a scrap of bleached cloth, and Antonio would suck that little clump of cloth with the look of someone who was sweetening life itself.

And, as there is nothing more beneficial than the effect of one day following another, Antonio gradually became healthier every day.

The house was made of adobe bricks, full of doors and windows that opened onto a large cor-ral with lots of shade and various tones of green.

The whitewashed exterior welcomed the wind, the sun, the moon, the family. In the living room, plump portraits of the ancestors swung under the protection of the hearts of Jesus and Mary. There was Grandfather with his glasses and cane, Great-grandmother among flowers, Father as a young man with his moustache and a bow tie that the children called the butterfly tie.

Made of running boards, the floor was the same age as the house, but many repairs had been made in wood of other colours or from bits of tins of Colombo marmalade. Several of the bedrooms, their beds covered with woven spreads, opened onto the hallway, where earthenware swallows flew along the walls.

In the dining room was a huge table with wicker chairs. In a corner sat a crystal cabinet with its sparkling glasses, chalices and decanters. On the other side of the room was the clay filter beaded with fresh water fetched from the mine — water that mysteriously sprung up between stones and roots. From this room you could see the kitchen with its wood stove and more shelves, decorated with newspaper clippings, where spotless jars and cans held sweets and meringues.

The house was a part of the countryside. It appeared to have been born there among the mango trees, with the brook bubbling through the yard, wetting the feet of the jaboticaba trees.

The vegetable and flower gardens were combined. Rose petals would often sleep among the lettuce leaves. Sometimes strawberries would interlace themselves among the tomato stalks. The papayas were shared with the birds, who didn't ask for permission—fitting behaviour for those who indicated the passing of time with songs and warbling.

Nothing grew out of its place. Even sedge grass sprang up, intermingling with the stones at the base of the house. These old stones were dressed in moss that provided velvet for the baby lambs in the Christmas nativity scene.

The clothes hanging out on the line revealed the direction of the winds and etched colours against the green fields that stretched out until they touched the sky.

This was how Antonio's family lived. They chose to be in this part of the wide world, receiving messages of life through nature, learning with the seasons, changes, loss, the grafting of plants. They followed the flowerings, pruned trees during certain phases of the moon and spoke little of other delights.

In March the rainy season bade farewell with the floods of St. Jose, which invaded the fields and killed the cattle. Then April arrived, tingeing the blue sky from tip to tip. The dawns became more transparent. The sun, following the line of the roof tiles, drew pictures on the little girls inside the house.

In the middle of April, Antonio caught whooping cough, which got worse and worse. He lost his breath and began to choke and turn purple. His mother complained that this new affliction hit him just at the time when he had gained a little more weight. The illness worried both Antonio's parents and his brother and sisters, who had already been dreaming of playing with him.

As a rule, Mother got up very early, just before the sun came out. With Antonio in her arms, she would pass through the smell given off by the corral, a remedy recommended to cure a lengthy cough. His brother and sisters would go along on this walk. They would try to teach their brother to breathe in the aroma of the awakening yard, while the chickens, surrounded by chicks, cackled and combed the area for small insects.

Before the sun warmed up the world too much, Mother would return to the house. She would leave Antonio on the wooden floor, which had been washed with cactus leaves. It was time to soak the rice — not before picking out any bugs in it — and poke the fire to cook the beans. And the boy, caught in the square traced on the floor by the sun streaming through the window, would spend hours watching the trail of ants or the flight of birds in the blue outside.

When night came, Father would plunge a horseshoe into the hot coals of the stove. Then he would fling it red-hot into a jug of milk. Antonio's patient mother would give him small swallows of the ferrous milk, in the hope that it would soften his cough.

Afterwards, they would put out the lamps with puffs of breath or fingers dampened with spit. The smell of the kerosene would penetrate into the roof and as far as the stars. The only sound to be heard was the straw of the mattresses as each of them, now alone, would try to get comfortable in order to welcome their dreams.

The silence, clothed in darkness, would watch over the world. Only a bird's cheep broke the silence, and then only rarely.

Dawn would arrive between the rooster's song and the mooing of the cows. Mother, already in the kitchen, would be preparing the corn cake, which was baked in a covered pan among the coals. The smell would permeate the whole house and awaken the children, who imagined pieces of cheese melting between the slices.

Father, at this hour, had already left through the fields and roads, carrying milk or charcoal or hauling firewood.

In this way life grew old without anyone noticing it.

Antonio's whooping cough went away. He no longer coughed or spent his mornings in the corral. He was still protected by blue flannelette shirts printed with innocent flowers and clown faces, however.

But suddenly, he had a very high fever, which was constantly measured by the backs of hands placed against his forehead. With the help of the neighbours, his mother would plunge her boy into a basin of stingingly cold water, then wrap him in huge blankets to bring down the fever. No one knew the cause, so they suspected everything. Sadness began to surround the house; it was obvious even in the faces of the other children. Father stayed nearby in the yard in case of an emergency, and did not go to the field to work.

After about three days, when the boy was getting very weak, everything cleared up. Antonio, thin, with his tiny arms and legs, turned over a jaboticaba branch, as if by magic. But now his body was covered with chickenpox! The others, who were not allowed to come close to their brother, watched his impatient scratching from a distance.

It was on this occasion that his godmother spoke for the first time.

"If you had given him an elderberry tea," she said, "this illness would have broken up much earlier."

But Antonio survived. A few days later he was once again as calm as a tree after it has given fruit—open and ready for a new flowering.

Father arrived one afternoon looking like a hero, with a live armadillo in a sack. Mother cleaned the aluminum basin until it looked like silver. Her husband bled the animal with a sharp knife, and the blood fell thickly into the basin.

Antonio was placed in the basin naked while the blood was still warm, and his mother's hands spread it all over his body.

While she did this, she said, "You will never have a skin disease again. You will grow up forever clear of boils, chickenpox, measles or German measles."

The children, watching closely, were learning the law of things. Their mother and father were their first teachers. They knew things that could only have been read or heard from very wise people who lived in kingdoms of springtime.

It seems that illness is just a child's attempt to find a way of staying in the world. If it isn't pains in the stomach, it's in the ears, or colds that threaten pneumonia. If Antonio needed more attention than most children, it was because he was born before his time. Just when everyone thought that he would spend another two months inside his mother, he leapt into life. And though he surprised everyone, his own fright at encountering everyone else's surprise must have been even greater. His timidity must have been born there. After all, he entered the world without permission, disrupting everything. It is likely that the first words he ever heard were, "I didn't think he'd make it, but finally he did. This lively boy is stubborn."

Time brought Antonio's first birthday. The fine rain sounded like seeds the sky was planting noisily on the roof. Wandering among the flower beds, a fancy umbrella in her hand, Mother gathered flowers for the house: calla lilies, dahlias, wild roses.

On the tables the starched tablecloths, embroidered with cross-stitches and needlepoint crochet, announced that there would be guests.

The grandparents arrived the night before and helped to get the house ready. Grandmother, stretching out the sheets, would make butterflies with the covers at the foot of each bed — butterflies woven with cotton gathered and carded at home. Grandfather, with Antonio on his knee, would tell stories: "Where's that little bacon who was here? The cat ate him. Where's the cat . . ." Whether or not Antonio understood all the details, he grasped the tales through the hugs and smiles that went back and forth between himself and his grandfather.

In the pantry, there were trays covered with cashews, cookies and milk sweets. These were coloured in various tones of indigo and cut in squares, rectangles and diamond shapes. Sweets made of papaya root reminded you of coconut candies. The fruit trees were full of candies wrapped in tissue paper that had been shredded and curled up at the ends with the edge of scissors.

In the afternoon, the family, all freshly bathed and wearing their party clothes, would smile for the neighbours and relatives who were arriving. And with them came presents for Antonio: the latest fine cotton, silk socks, small soap boxes, tins of talcum powder, small medals to wear on chains.

The plates of sweets made the rounds of the room. Mother also served liqueurs made of figs and cherries. She apologized for the elaborateness of the party, but insisted that Antonio deserved it.

And the children — brother and sisters, cousins, friends — savouring glasses of red currant juice, their mouths tinged with red, would glance quickly at their parents, looking for permission to eat just one more sweet, or to take one more fruit ball from the table in the centre of the room.

The proud father, with Antonio in his arms, came up with a few words for each guest. He would talk about the weather, future harvests, the new animals and the risk of floods, but he never attempted to hide his great happiness, which Antonio also felt.

The godparents were the last to take their leave. They said goodbye under a fine rain, blessing their godson. They departed with a plate full of assorted sweets covered with a lace towel, with which they would continue celebrating Antonio's birthday the following day.

The grandparents' visit always managed to stretch out birthdays for a few more days. They never stayed for a short time since their journey was long. They went part of the way by train, between whistles, fumes and the smell of lemon-scented verbena at the edge of the track. The other part was by bus, their baggage tied to the roof with rope and covered with canvas. The passengers would chew on matches so as not to be sick.

Grandfather would arrive with a dust jacket over his black three-piece suit. Grandmother, with a scarf on her head, would complain about the dust and the distance. They always said it was their last journey, since they were no longer healthy enough to travel such a long way. After bringing up eleven children, it was time for a rest.

They arrived full of news of uncles, aunts, cousins, grandchildren and great-grandchildren. The grandparents' house in the city had become the resting place for the whole family. It had been bought with the grand prize money won in a lottery. Grandfather had left the countryside and his coffee plantation and set up house in the city. Dressed in his black suit and dark tie, he leaned out the window, watching the passersby on Patience Street, wishing everyone good morning, good afternoon, good evening. He never worked again.

During this long visit, Grandmother, sitting on the bed on the chamber pot covered by her full skirt, told stories of headless mules, souls from the other world and werewolves.

The grandchildren listened, full of fear yet hoping to have a chance to meet a suffering soul.

Nights were shorter when their grandparents were visiting. The children went to bed later, after the stories, the news and a bowl of maize flour and milk. One of the children always asked if there would be another birthday tomorrow or how many days their grandparents were going to stay. Father would interrupt the conversation and make the children leave their grandparents in peace.

Then there would be a chorus of voices saying, ''Bless Mother, bless Father, bless Grandmother, bless Grandfather.''

''Don't forget the guardian angel,'' Mother would add.

Love was very silent. You could see it in the way Mother carefully rinsed the clothes in blue washing powder. It was silent, but you could see love in her fingers as she cut the curly kale, took the leaves off the cabbage, candied figs or embroidered cinnamon flowers on the rice pudding in the bowls.

You could read love in Father's strong body, in his enjoyment of his work, in his gentleness throughout the long Sundays. It was silent, but you could hear love murmuring in the couple's bedroom at night. The house, which had no ceiling, allowed this murmuring to escape with the smell of smoke and cinnamon that invaded sheets and uncertainties, and was later filtered out through the roof tiles.

Mother and Father would test this love when, seated in the heat of the kitchen, they would speak

of distances, of grandparents, of origins, of lov-
ers and of weddings.

And, when sleep approached, it was love that
would carry each child in its arms to bed, and
arrange the blanket underneath his or her chin.

The Vitality
of Nine O'Clock

No one had to bathe Antonio in scalding monkey water to make him clever. A few days after his first birthday, he began to walk. He had crawled earlier, pulling himself up by table legs and the edges of beds. Now he was no longer imprisoned by the block of sunshine coming through the window. He would run through the house to greet his father when he arrived home from work. He ran for his mother's lap when she sat down on one of the steps leading into the yard.

But now the work was doubled, his mother said. Any carelessness on her part and the boy would be out in the rain, playing with leaves and twigs carried by the floods. His mother would lift Antonio up by his arms, bring him in and sit him at the table in the dining room. She would rub alcohol on his chest, dress him in dry clothing and lament the fact that she had let his umbilical cord be thrown into the stream.

One day his godmother, an observant woman who had mothered many children, remarked that Antonio was slow in learning how to talk. He walked, ate the same food as the rest of the family, slept without needing anyone's help, and yet he still did not know how to say a single word.

According to his godmother, he needed to drink water gathered in the church bell on a rainy day. It was a sacred remedy. It was believed that rain water from the church bell had the power to aid one's speech, and it had the added advantage that the boy would also learn to speak at the right moments. And so they did what she said. Antonio did not refuse. He drank the sonorous water from the heavens with the same alacrity as one eats the crumbs of a cake.

No one knows if it was the bell water, the godmother's faith or the timing, but sure enough, Antonio began to talk. But to everyone's surprise, he talked without stopping, independently of everything, just as gossips do.

He answered the questions of mangos, he talked to the plants, he spoke the language of the crickets and the streams. He even dreamed out loud.

Once again his godmother came, this time to say that her godson did not have a trained ear. You could say whatever you liked, but he only heard what he wanted to hear. His father already called him a *tiu*, an insect with no hearing. But he said this in such a sweet way that Antonio listened affectionately and then continued talking, as indifferent to the criticism as a sulky cow.

And so from his godmother, possessor of so many recipes, came the suggestion of putting cloves of garlic soaked in warm castor oil into the boy's ears. But Antonio, now smelling of baked rice, continued speaking and hearing only the noises he liked to hear—of water, wind, leaf, bird, silence and storm.

As Antonio grew older, he also grew in love. Now more than a year old and with a firm body, he would extend his arms, offering himself to the world. He was not afraid of anyone. He gave the impression that he had always been very healthy, even to those who did not know him. Antonio became very gentle. He hardly ever cried, and with the tip of his finger he would gently caress the eyes, ears, mouth or nose of whoever carried him.

Those who were able to see felt on seeing him for the first time that he was a disarming boy fit just for affection. His way of looking at things, his ability to offer himself up or to lean against others, his way of nestling in their arms, made people want to smother him in warmth. They would squeeze him with hugs and bury him in their hearts. It seemed almost to be a kind of envy. Everyone wanted to be loved the way he was.

In spite of his affectionate nature and trans-parent sweetness, no one risked calling him Tony or any other nickname. They called him Antonio, using their whole mouth. They said his name from the inside, as if they wanted to preserve everything there was of him and were unwilling to divide him up into pieces.

It was a name decided upon quickly, because of the fear he would go to limbo, but it was also a homage to a dear saint. And this name came to be the only one that served for this lovable boy who was born in a hurry, ahead of his time, yet resistant to death. No one knew if he was like the saint or like the boy in the saint's arms. This uncertainty brought Antonio close to the angels.

When it was cold at night, the children would play in the house so as not to catch the cool night air. Father and Mother would warm themselves in the heat of the kitchen. At times, the only noise was the rattling of the plate that covered the pan of beans on the stove.

Mother had a crocodile purse with a silver clasp hidden in her clothes closet. Inside an envelope in the purse, among certificates, registration forms, portraits and pictures of the saints, was the green glass eye of the grandfather who had died long before Antonio was born.

The children would gaze at the eye and then, possessed by fear, run to the kitchen. They would lie in their mother's lap and grab their father's legs, breathing quick breaths until the fear disappeared. Then everything would begin all over again. Step by step, their bodies tense, they would slowly go into their mother's bedroom without making the slightest sound. They would open the purse and take out the envelope. The grandfather's green glass eye was open, not sleeping, and it stared at them without blinking. The children, who wanted to be scared, were frightened once again. They would run back to the kitchen immobilized by terror, seeking their parents' warm arms.

The children's game brought back memories to Mother of her dead father and widowed mother. Sometimes she would try to lessen the children's fear, saying, "It's not worth being afraid of the dead. It makes more sense to be afraid of the living. The soul of your grandfather is happy there in the heavens. His eye doesn't see. It's only a souvenir."

The children knew little of their grandfather's story. They would listen to some words about him when the family got together: crime, prison, jealousy, betrayal.

But the grandfather's spying eye was not the only thing he'd left behind. There were other mementos: the cane with the silver handle, the black hat, the tie, and even his pride so visible in the body of their mother.

Antonio imagined his grandfather in the sky, looking at God with just one eye. The other did not sleep, even in his mother's purse.

Little by little Antonio came to understand the secrets of the world he was in. Everything was made up of so many surprises that he never thought about the other places that surely existed beyond the mountains.

He had no toys, so he made up games using fruits and seeds that he found on the paths leading to the barn, the corral, the stream or the cane field. Sometimes nature's magic provided a diversion. Antonio would daydream about the work of bees, about the huge loads that ants carried. He adored the licking love of the cows for their calves, the wasp hives in the corner of the roof that meant good luck, the flowers turning into fruit, the round stones that served as a mattress for the running water.

Now older and livelier, Antonio would run with his brother and sisters through the bush, looking for cricket corn, cherries and jujubes. They would climb up to the thinnest branches of trees, swing on barn doors, jump fences and chase fireflies with a burning stick.

Sometimes, sitting by the door of the house, they would wait for night to come and watch the birth of the first star. They didn't point at it for fear a wart would appear on the tip of their finger, but their hearts would recite, "The first star I see tonight, shall grant me everything I desire." Later, trying to find the Three Marias in the sky, they would long to grow up fast, to travel with their father to the country, to ride a horse, to take care of the cattle and be able to milk them. And the fear that nothing would turn out as he hoped would overwhelm Antonio.

At this hour the sky was so difficult to understand. It was so full of stars, yet so empty at the same time. Knowing that the dark of the night and the blue of the sky were made up of nothing made it all the more impossible to figure out.

Antonio was never lonely. He looked carefully at everything. And, seeing things slowly, he learned to live with their mysteries, not wanting to decipher things for fear they would lose their enchantment.

They say that the boy who plays with fire wets his bed every night. Once Antonio heard this, he never again grabbed a burning stick to chase fireflies. He began to make a big effort. He didn't drink anything, even water, after dinner. But at dawn it was always the same thing: he would wake up with a strong and wet warmth running between his legs.

In the morning, you could see his mattress set out in the sun and his bedsheets being soaked. This increased the shame imprinted on his face.

A rattlesnake has a rattle on its tail. The rattle is a set of horny rings that produce the snake's *scheek*, *scheek* sound. They say that each ring represents a year in the poisonous snake's life, so that if there are seven of them, the snake is seven years old.

They learned from their mother, not their godmother this time, that wearing a rattlesnake rattle tied around the neck would stop a child from urinating in bed. It wasn't long before Mr. Olegario killed a snake in the field. Mother hung the rattle, along with a medal, around Antonio's neck. The boy walked slowly, afraid that the sound would summon another rattlesnake. He knew that the rattlesnake bites and that its victim dies from lack of air. In addition, one rattlesnake is always accompanied by another.

It was at this same time that a scorpion bit Antonio in the middle of his leg. His mother got a little black brick made out of the powdered horn of a bush deer, wet it in milk and placed it on the bite. The little brick stuck. The pain was so bad that Antonio screamed and seemed to be dying. After a long time, with his mother wiping his sweat with cold water, the little brick fell off. She picked up a jar of milk and threw the brick in it, and showed Antonio that the milk had turned dark. The poison had been sucked up by the brick.

But what finally made Antonio stop urinating in bed was his experience with bats. His father had told him that the rat, when it gets very old, wants to have wings. It turns into a bat—the bird of the devil—which feeds itself by eating blood and, as it only flies in the dark, is guided by smell.

In that house without a ceiling, Antonio would cover his head and go to sleep overcome by his fear of bats. His dreams changed.

His mother took the rattle from around his neck and put it away, saying, "Someone else might need it. It is not just the days that come one after the other. So do brothers and sisters."

Antonio's father, a quiet man, was always scratching his head, as if caressing his thoughts. He worked hard and with hardly any rest. There was always a wire to tighten, a chicken whose wings needed cutting, a plank in the corral that needed another nail, a plant that needed propping up to grow straighter. On Sunday he would sit under the shade of a tree and be alone with time, which gave him some calm.

He didn't talk much, though at times he told short tales. One was about a chicken that ran under his truck. There was no way he could avoid killing it. The little chicks stayed, cheeping around their dead mother. As there was nothing else he could do, he gathered up the chicks and brought them into the house. Today, when he drives, he isn't afraid of bridges, ditches or cattle-guards. But if he sees a chicken with her chicks, he uses his brakes.

Taking up the silence once again, Father would open his very sharp penknife, pick up the tobacco, roll a cigarette and smoke. Antonio wouldn't ask any questions and his father wouldn't respond. It was a very heavy silence.

Antonio's sisters, who had already begun to dress like angels in coronation caps and had won packets of almond sweets, stood behind their father, combing and uncombing his hair, pulling at it again and again. Father must have liked the attention, because he would look around without moving his head, so as not to stop the game.

From time to time he would travel for a few days. Mother would lock up the doors and windows earlier, leaning axes and tubs against them. Her fear reminded them that Father was away. When he returned he would bring bread and salami wrapped in brown paper. At home there were often cookies and cakes, but bread was something from another world. And the red salami, cut in rounds, with half moons of pepper, tasted like the love that Father expressed in his gestures but didn't say out loud.

He had some old books that he was always rereading. They were the stories of famous people. Sometimes, using a quill and ink, he would write his name, the names of his children and his wife in beautiful letters. Antonio, who didn't know how to read, was very curious to know where his name appeared on the sheet of paper — whether it was close to or far away from his father's name. Without daring to put the question, he would ask his father to rewrite his name at least one more time. His father would go along with the boy's curiosity, putting even more effort into forming the letters. Antonio would double his attention.

The following day, Mother would start the fire with the paper, burning the names without thinking of Antonio, who had wanted to hide the writings to copy some day. From there came his wish to have a drawer with a lock.

In the west where the sun set, sometimes hearts were transformed into resting places by sadness. The sadness would arrive with the breeze between colours and silence and go as far as Mother's arms, folded on her lap. Then her eyes, full of tears, would reach across landscapes that Antonio knew nothing of.

Father, leaning over his knees, was defence-less in the light of a visit so serene, but that ruthlessly unfurled old names, deep shadows, huge frontiers of desire. And Antonio could read everything in his wrinkles, in the creasing of his brow.

His father's sadness contaminated everyone. They all stayed away from him, hoping to go to sleep earlier and in repose find a revealing dream. But they surmised nothing, except per-haps that sadness was also possible.

The Fullness of Noon

MOTHER began to fatten the chickens. In her spare time she would embroider bunches of simple flowers on small pieces of cloth. On others she would make hems, counting threads, cutting and unravelling the fine cotton. Her happiness was evident in the embroideries.

While she was visiting a neighbour, she would say things that Antonio didn't understand.

"I think it's going to be sometime in September."

"Yes. I'm favouring the colour pink. I dreamt of a girl."

"It will be Anna, after my mother-in-law."

One night they moved Antonio into his brother's bedroom. They apologized, but said that he was already a boy and hardly fit in the cradle anymore. And it's true he had been sleeping all curled up. Even so, his heart tightened, suspecting something.

His godmother, passing her hand over his head, was saying other mysterious things.

"You will no longer be the youngest child."

"You won't be the one to scrape the bowl anymore."

During this move to another bedroom, Antonio got to know the guardian angel. Hanging on the white wall above the headboard of the bed was a pink painting. It was a print that showed a very high mountain, almost boring into the sky, with dark clouds and lightning depicting tempests. At the bottom was a precipice that froze the soul. A boy, in shoes and socks, crossed a narrow and dangerous path at the top of the mountain. His face showed fear mixed with caution. One false move would mean death. But perched on the boy's back was God's angel, diligent and guarding, protecting the crossing with arms and wings. His robe was of the reddest rose, his eyes blue. Everything was of a beauty that merited faith.

Antonio's confidence in the guardian angel grew to such an extent that he could now walk on top of the roof or cross mountain streams, balancing himself on mud-covered rocks and tree trunks left by the floods. But he did everything without looking back. He was afraid of seeing the angel face to face. He knew there were things that it was not worth the trouble to see. Just believing was enough—like in the stork that was going to bring him a new brother or sister.

The house swelled with the sound of a new cry. It came accompanied by the smell of parsley that invaded the rooms, announcing the soup made from a fat chicken. Antonio liked eating the wings, the part infused most strongly with herbs. He didn't like the feet. The problem was that he couldn't eat just one foot. The chicken raked around with one foot and gathered up its food with the other, so it was said that those who ate only one foot risked not being able to gather anything, just scattering things, and of being poor for the rest of their lives.

Anna was born at the right time, without upsetting anyone's life. Antonio greeted her lovingly, and was there for the burial of her umbilical cord close to the dahlias. She would be beautiful and a good gardener. But it was on this day that he learned that his umbilical cord had been seized by the floods. This made him afraid of being abandoned.

The fear completely arrested his body and dulled his nature, floating in the waters of his eyes, rootless. It wasn't the same fear he had had of the guardian angel. It was a fear of what he, a boy of the flowing waters, would come to be. A fear that ached without relief. A fear that his thoughts would become a reality.

The visitors arrived. Mother told everyone that after five years, they had thought Antonio would be the last child. They talked about the baptism, the celebration, the godparents and the ironed cloth for the holy ceremony. Anna would be dedicated to St. Anne.

Antonio's godmother, now more responsible for him, did not waste words: "You will have to be a very good boy. You must not make extra work for your mother. She has a small daughter to take care of now. You will have to help out by not bothering or worrying her."

In these kindly words, Antonio heard that he was not a good boy. Soon he was spending time on his own, always in the corners of the house talking to himself. For the first time, he sensed that living required not understanding.

His father saw that Antonio had a tendency to be around the adults and discreetly listen to their conversations. The boy would stay in a corner of the room keeping himself amused with some small ball or toy. Sometimes he would be underneath the table, sorting stones or counting seeds. His father was proud of his son's curiosity, the fact that he always wanted to know more things, to see everything from all sides.

He loved that boy who was born unexpectedly and survived only because he was so stubborn. Thinking Antonio's life to be a miracle, he prepared a mixture of quinine, magnesium, cinnamon, rhubarb and muscatel wine. He left the bottle on the kitchen tray where Antonio was to take spoonfuls of it first thing every morning in order to grow stronger.

Oranges, mangos, avocados, pomegranates and papayas were fruits that Antonio knew. One day he came to know the apple, red as a cock's comb and smooth as the porcelain cups his mother had received as a wedding gift. The apples came wrapped in purple paper, the colour of the Virgin's robe—she who had the seven swords of grief. The apple's strong smell meant you could never eat one unawares. A real fruit, exaggerated in colour and smell, it openly announced its presence.

To learn how to swim, the boys would swallow live minnows. Antonio didn't waste any time. With water up to his waist and a small sieve, he swallowed all the minnows he had caught. A tickle in the throat and another in the stomach and he was already imagining himself diving deep to the bottom of the water among cities and kingdoms.

Instead, he caught an intestinal infection, causing fever and general bodily depression. He vomited frequently. After many teas had had no effect, his father left for the city. He explained everything to a pharmacist and returned weighed down with potions, fortifiers, capsules and another package of apples.

Seated quietly by the window, following a special diet, Antonio smelled the purple paper and ate the apples, which reminded him of prayers. In a light and lazy state, with the stomach that had once been an aquarium, he thought of what must exist beyond the mountains: cities, forests, rivers, seas. Ah! The sea made of salt water that didn't even taste of tears. So large that it had only one bank. Even more, it had waves, like those on the picture on the wall, coloured a blue borrowed from the sky. How hard it was for a boy who knew only the small streams with their floods and droughts to imagine the ocean!

Besides the ducks, a few turkeys and some regular chickens, they kept leghorn chickens in the yard — elegant white queens crowned by ruby-red silhouetted combs. They were good layers. When they slept — with the sun setting — they were like silver ballerinas, immobile on one foot. They made their nests in the banana trees, among shade and branches, as if someone was threatening them with attack.

The children often made a game of hunting for their eggs. Quick as cats, watchful as the fowl that foretold the dawns, they went around the thickets and stumps looking for nests.

Although very sure of what he was looking for, Antonio became frightened when actually confronted with a nest. When he got close to it, his hands would tremble and his heart would balk. He felt as if he were robbing something that was still in the process of happening. Taking the eggs meant not allowing the bursting forth of the babies that he could hear inside the shells, hoping to be born in due time with their mother's warmth. Time that he himself had not waited.

And the chickens were so clearly suspicious. The most wonderful thing was how they pretended they were eating when they were not, how they pecked the food and let it fall to show the chicks where the food was. He'd been taught that once you found a nest you always had to leave behind at least one egg — the nest egg — so that the chicken would continue to lay. But Antonio always wanted to gather the nest egg as well. Then the chicken, losing the location of the nest, who knows, would build another, someplace farther away, more hidden, more secret.

Then one morning she would appear surrounded by a band of chicks, protecting them under her wings — the ballerina's parasol — with her bristly love.

Mother would play with her children on the long and peaceful Sunday afternoons.

At the foot of the stairs, next to the kitchen door, was the water tank. Made of grey cement, it held cold water that ran from the hill, a crystalline spring running through a bamboo pipe. All around there, the humidity supported the growth of green moss, carpets where the ants passed by dragging piles of leaves. Just looking at it you felt caressed by such fine velvet.

Mother would colour the water of the tank with food colouring, one colour at a time, and would plunge the pure white leghorn chickens into a coloured bath of blue, green, yellow, red or purple. In a short time the farm, as if by miracle, looked like a castle courtyard peopled by rare birds drawn from fairy tales. Everything was under a spell. There was no book, even those that came from far away, with a more beautiful story than the one Mother knew how to tell. It wasn't hard for Antonio to imagine himself a prince and the son of magicians.

As the sun set between the valleys and mountains, that harmless band of chickens would perch on the branches of trees like a rainbow of ballerinas at a carnival. Antonio would watch the branches as long as he could, its old inhabitants wearing their new party dresses, thinking of the Christmas tree that would soon sprout in the corner of the living room, sheltering presents in its shadow.

The next day, the sound of maize in the feeder would present the children with a hungry rainbow already half fading because of the night's cool air. But the children knew that their mother, at any moment, would begin to play at something else.

They said that Jose, the oldest child, was already grown up, a man. He wore long pants to school and helped his father with the work.

Seated in the driver's seat of the truck, he seemed to be convinced that he was the boss. He even started saying swine instead of pig and live-stock instead of cows. He was always trying to be another father in his brother's life.

Jose would soon be leaving for the city, where he would take an exam and get his primary school diploma. He was obsessed with arithmetic and grammar. He leafed through Father's books just to make the others envious and read out loud any arithmetic solution that he came across. He no longer lunched with his brother and sisters seated on the bench in the kitchen. He made up his own plate, choosing the largest piece of meat. At night he stayed with the adults or listened to the ''Voice of Brazil'' on the battery-powered radio with his father. From time to time, his face full of foam, he would vainly but unceremoniously use his father's razor. Then Antonio would look around the room and ask, "We have another father in this house, don't we?"

Antonio had three older siblings: Jose and two sisters. The girls wore ribbons — butterflies of cloth—in their hair and were always dressed the same, in calico dresses and bibs. They liked Antonio at certain times: when he climbed into the guava tree and picked the guavas highest up or killed wild doves for them to eat, or when he washed the chicken innards to make sausages. They also went to school. Always full of new ideas, they said they wanted to be teachers. They played at teaching Antonio, who would stay seated as they wrote on the wall with pieces of charcoal and gave him orders and more orders: sit down, be quiet, don't look to the side, careful, watch out or we'll punish you. They repeated things that Antonio didn't understand but paid a lot of attention to — dictation, silent reading, reading out loud, copying, composition.

The worst was the singing class:

> Everything provides an excuse
> for Lily not to go to school.
> Yesterday it was a sore tooth
> today she lost her purse.
> The other day it was that snack
> that was badly prepared.

> Instead of a milk sweet
> Her mother gave her guava jam.

They would yell all the way through it—louder, still louder—and Antonio would open his mouth to the world, singing without knowing why and would still get only fifty per cent.

In poetry class, the sisters would test his memory. He would learn by heart verses that the girls pounded into his ears like a carpenter's hammer—''Three on each side, author unknown'':

> In the window a young lady
> was working on her embroidery
> Six ringlets had she
> three on each side
> A young man passed by
> elegant and well dressed was he
> with six moustache strands
> three on each side
> Seeing the girl embroidering
> he immediately fell in love
> and gave her six kisses
> three on each side
> Her father saw the whole thing
> came down the staircase angrily
> and beat him six times with a cane
> three on each side.

There were soft cardboard dolls, covered with a pink dough that you couldn't get wet or they would cave in. They would come dressed in crêpe paper, their maroon hair undulating, huge and so ugly that they would need new clothes. The sisters decided to hold a baptism and invited Antonio to be the godfather. He wore his new white pants, so important did he think the invitation. But the red currants from the party got all over them. Antonio, afraid of getting into trouble with his mother, hid behind the house and tried to cover up the stains with lime left over from whitewashing the house. It only made things worse. And when he timidly came back into the house, his mother said he had gotten his pants dirty just to irritate her. This day the injustice hurt.

Antonio went to bed. He thought of leaving home and looking for his umbilical cord all over the world. His heart tightening, he felt homesick for the sea, and he licked the salt of his tears in the dark.

The children learned how to play from their mother. She would do everything to make them more cheerful. If the way was long, she would play at counting the fence posts, at running behind their shadows, at jumping fences, at walking in the rhythm of the slaves. Playing always shortened the path, she would say. If the wall was high, the one who got there first was the most beautiful and would see angels, she would shout, already skipping towards it. And it was always she who arrived first. If she ran out of stories, she would look at the sky and make up characters from there. Antonio remembered Grandfather's green glass eye.

While making cookies, Mother would give bits of the dough to the children. Each of them would make animals or fruits: rabbits, oranges, snakes, armadillos, dolls, puppies. Then she would bake or fry them, asking, ''Do you want the dolls blond or brown-haired?''

This is how she taught the children to make and eat the national flag, when there was no meat. She served plates of green chayote, cooked in spring water, rice and a fried egg. She would explain that the plate contained the green of the mountains, and if you mixed the rice with the egg yoke, you could make the gold. The plate was enamelled with blue, so everything was ready.

Thus Antonio learned to make the Brazilian flag—his first drawing. He was helped in this by Jose, who at these times wasn't measuring efforts and knowledge. According to the older brother, you could even make the flag's stars with grains of white rice. The strip of order and progress was made with a border of egg white.

And when it was ready, they would ask, "Is it beautiful, Mother?"

"Very pretty," she would say.

"Then I'm going to eat it . . ."

"Don't forget that each part has its own flavour," she would say.

So that cold flag became something tastier than all other foods. Knowing and eating were things that went together.

"I've already eaten the mountains," one would cry.

"I'm going to eat the gold now," another would say.

"Now I'm going to eat the Southern Cross," the knowledgeable brother would say, in the tuneless voice of a young cock just before it becomes a rooster.

It was dawn—the hour at which the cocks tuned their throats and Father was getting ready to leave—when it slowly descended, like one who apologizes ahead of time. The children, who had been warned the night before, woke up from their sleep to enter into a nightmare. Each one received three spongy light-green capsules that looked like cookie dough. The smell was so strong that their noses couldn't stand it and quickly advised their stomachs, which were prepared to vomit with the arrival of the santa-maria worm remedy.

They swallowed it. They covered their heads with blankets and, thus entrenched, waited for the war. Those green bombs exploded in the stomach and the smell rose up into the throat, burning everything along the way. Even three days later the smell was still there, emanating from the skin.

But that wasn't the end of it. Two hours later each child took a large teaspoonful of castor oil. It was thick and the colour of honey and must have been made by wasps. The children could not get up until the remedy had had its "effect." The "effect" was a piercing stomach ache that cut from one side to the other and cooled you off down to your legs.

After this came a plate of thin maize meal with no bits of cheese or cinnamon, just to fool the stomach. Then the children could go out for some sun in the yard, waiting for new "effects," which would keep coming the whole morning.

One day, returning from a trip, Father brought home a bottle of pills called Surefire. He explained that the suffering caused by the santa-maria was no longer necessary. Once in a while they would take one or two of these pills, and they wouldn't need to rest or diet. Even the "effect" was unnoticeable.

Antonio felt relieved and had no doubts about the progress the world was making. Now what was needed, he thought, was to discover another medicine, sweeter and clearer, to take the place of cod liver oil. To get away once and for all from that milky bottle with a picture of a man carrying a fish on his back, and replace it with a nicer face.

Father cut palm leaves the night before. Sunday morning the whole family walked to the mass and procession. In the small chapel the women, wearing black and white veils, knelt with both knees on the benches. The men stayed on the sidelines, close to the paintings of the stations of the cross, kneeling on just one knee. Antonio, close to his father, imitated his movements. Once the mass was over, the procession went along dusty paths around the chapel. Everyone prayed and sang with leaves in their hands:

> Sacred Heart
> You will reign.
> You will always be
> my sweet delight.

And everything ended with the blessing of the branches.

Then the family would return to the house in mourning. Mother would hang the blessed leaves between the hearts of Jesus and Mary. If there was a storm at the time of the prayers for St. Barbara, they would burn the branches.

Sacred Week, the time of prayers, fasts and penance, was also a time of fear: demons, the headless mule, a soul from another world, spirits.

On the Thursday before Good Friday, Antonio would go with his father to the river. Father would patiently play the hook while the boy squirmed and waited for victory. Antonio would then secure a fork to hang the fish by the neck. There were lots of different fish, and although they were small, after a few hours Antonio would have a stack the size of a bunch of bananas.

With the sun at its height, Father would put down the rod and put the lid on the bait. Then he would take the lemonade, two metal mugs, hard-boiled eggs, pieces of cake, cottage cheese and sweets out of the haversack. They would eat slowly, in tune with the laziness of the day. On the way back, Antonio would ride on his father's shoulders, looking at the world from on high.

On Good Friday, they couldn't listen to the radio, cut their nails, sweep the house, speak loudly or sing. Sin surrounded them. The only sound was that of the hot oil in which Mother fried the fish after dipping them in maize meal. But they were allowed to plant garlic in already prepared beds, where they would spring up more quickly.

The rest of the day was divided between memories of the saints covered in purple cloth in the chapel, the fear of the devil dressed up as a rich and handsome young man and the big moon in the sky watching over everything. On Saturday the hallelujahs broke out. Everything returned to its place except for the suffering of Christ.

One afternoon, Father arrived home with a worried look on his face. He took a bath and shaved without saying much. He didn't turn on the radio to hear the "Voice of Brazil." You could tell from the silence that something was about to happen. After a long wait, he took a half-crushed letter from his pocket and began to read it to everyone:

> My dear son,
> I hope that this letter will find you and all of your family enjoying health and happiness. I am always thinking of you and ask God to spread his blessing on everyone in your house.
> I received the custard you sent and the preserved mangos, which your mother loves very much. They arrived along with your letter, for which I thank you very much. I didn't respond at the time because the delivery man was in a hurry. Don't forget that

during the mango season, children often get boils. It is good to give them a Glauber salt laxative and a basil ointment to heal them more quickly. You should squeeze the boils until the hard bit comes out. It hurts, but the pain goes away quickly.

But my letter is to tell you that your mother isn't in good health. She has a lot to complain about. Her feet are very swollen and she has a high fever that doesn't go away. She is in bed and we still haven't found the right medicines. I know that she would love to have you visit her, because she always speaks about you and everyone in your family with a lot of affection.

Accept your parents' blessing and give my regards to all.

Your father,
Joaquim

"We should get the children ready and go tomorrow, very early. There isn't much time," Mother said.

"I've already asked Mr. Olegario to look after the house and take care of the new animals," Father responded.

When his parents returned a few days later, Antonio knew about death and the burden of the living. Mother, wearing black clothing, had sewn strips of black cloth onto the sleeves of Father's shirts. Death buried lightheartedness for a long time.

While the cold left frost on the streams and on the fields, the angels' wings would enjoy the sun at the edges of the windows. Angel dresses of white satin were ironed with a red-hot iron while the sisters waited each night with their hair wrapped in paper rollers.

Almonds were the food of angels. Mother would bathe toasted almonds in sugar in a pan on the fire. Little by little they would be dressed in sweet white robes to go with the month, the holiday and the saint.

At the end of the afternoon, fit out in baskets, the packets of almonds in crêpe paper would be the angels' evening meal after the crowning of the Virgin.

On the altar, with long staircases on each side, Mary would await her crown and her palm in the rain of rose petals.

Father brought pairs of batteries, bits of wire and small lamps. He wrapped the wire in the girls' crowns with the lamps soldered at the tip. The batteries were placed in cloth bags that Mother sewed under the sisters' — that is, the angels' — arms.

At the hour of the coronation, between songs and solos, the lights of the church were put out. The sisters with their illuminated crowns looked like real angels. And the faithful would say together:

> Oh, come, let us go
> with flowers to meet the challenge.
> With flowers to Mary
> the Virgin mother of God.
> Oh, come, let us go
> with flowers to Mary
> Bless with happiness
> the Virgin mother of God.

Afterwards, the angels would receive their paper bags and at night they would walk around the house eating the pearls of sugar. It was a piece of the heavens that passed under Antonio's eyes.

It wasn't just the sun and the rains that determined the time. Each month was adorned with a festival according to the calendar that hung from the door in the dining room. In October they would dance with bells on their ankles and mirrored hats. In January was the festival of the Three Kings. And with June came the flagpole, bonfire, square dance and the thirteen days of prayer.

Everything began on the first day of the month. The decorated altar would be installed in the living room, where the picture of the saint and his child would be surrounded by coloured paper flowers.

The neighbours and the relatives would get together to say the rosary and the litanies. Afterwards they would drink coffee and eat the blessed bread of St. Antonio.

Days ahead of time, Mother would busy herself preparing the snacks. She would kindle the oven's coals with a straw fan while covering its opening with a piece of roof tile rolled up in a banana leaf to conserve the heat. Trays full of various sweets announced that a lot of visitors were coming.

Father had put aside the blocks of wood to build the fire. He dug a hole to drive in the flagpole that would rise out of the fire and palm leaves.

The hot smell of rum, ginger and cinnamon was given off by the cauldrons next to pans of maize porridge and trays of Brazil nuts. Corn on the cob and potatoes baked in the bonfire helped to soften the cold.

If he happened to burn the tips of his fingers on the coals, Antonio was ready with the following speech: ''The fire has no cold, water has no thirst, air has no heat, bread has no hunger. St.

Lawrence, cure these burns with the power that God has given you.''

That night the young women dreamed of weddings and promised to cook the saint in the beans, drown him in the coffee water or put him in the strainer along with the coffee grounds. Others threatened to capture their young man and only let him go after the wedding.

It was a time dressed in calico, bright patches and hats, with hopes of meetings and the certainty of the saint's protection. The rest of the month belonged to St. John, St. Peter and St. Anne. Then July would arrive, bringing holidays, short visits to the godparents and nights of going to bed late.

It always rained in December. Mother fetched a roll of paper from the pantry and unrolled it on the wooden floor in the living room. She had crumbled charcoal and made glue out of flour. The children applied the glue to the paper and then stuck on pieces of charcoal with bits of mica to make it shine.

It was Christmas, as you could see from the nativity scene in the corner of the room. The bird seed had been planted to imitate a cultivated field and was now blooming in marmalade cans. White sifted sand covered the path taken by the pastors, the sheep and the Three Wise Men. The mirror for the lake was well polished, and the moss gathered from the spring was still green.

Gradually they set up the little mountain with foliage placed in pots hidden under paper. Later came the animals set between bushes, on top of stones and tall branches. All were invited: sheep, snakes, horses, giraffes, elephants, birds, puppies and even plastic ducks. At the door to the grotto was the red star placed next to the rooster, while inside were the Virgin, St. Joseph, the donkey and the ox. Gaspar, Melchior and Balthazar, the Three Kings, were on the highest point of the mountain. They arrived little by little, bringing presents that Antonio had never heard of, but that must have been precious: gold, frankincense and myrrh.

Mother made sweets, filled cans and preserved the meat in fat. Father arrived with small packages and hid them on top of the closets. None of the children asked any questions. Even Anna, who was still very small, knew that her father was Father Christmas.

On Christmas eve the children went to bed early while Mother arranged the king in the manger, the red ribbon in his open arms, ready to be kissed. In the morning they woke with the coffee table already in place: French toast, ring-shaped loaves, sweetmeats, fruitcakes. They received the presents from their father: apples, balloons, the Universal Globe almanac, the Tico-Tico comic book year-book, wooden trucks, dolls made of dough, shirts, pieces of cloth, balls, shoes, socks.

This year, Antonio was amazed to open a small wooden case with a sliding top. Inside there was a pencil sharpener, two pencils with erasers, a quill pen, white notebooks and a box of coloured pencils. In addition, a silver-coloured mug. All these things made him afraid of the year that they said was about to begin.

They arrived at school by roads, paths and short-cuts. It was a whitewashed room with windows on both sides and a floor covered with smooth cement. It seemed even more bare and clean because there was no ceiling. On the walls were huge paintings: a barefoot girl showing her shoes to the shoemaker, fishing with an old boot caught in the fishhook, geese menacingly approaching children and a huge coloured map. There was a blackboard on one of the walls and, close by, the teacher's desk covered with an embroidered cloth and a pot of flowers brought by the children. The pupils were divided into first, second, third and fourth classes at four big tables.

Outside was a covered courtyard with a wood fire, and a pitcher of cool water with a glass full of holes so that no one could dribble into it. On the other side was the garden where cabbage, pumpkins, okra, taro, green onions, celery, cassava and yams were grown. Farther along was the outhouse with the door turned towards the side of the mountain.

Surrounded by mountains on all sides, the school was attended by children who came from all directions. It was a quiet place, frequented only by the mooing of cattle, birds' songs, cries of the crickets and cicadas and the honks of the trucks far away on the highway.

Antonio arrived in a new uniform of navy blue cotton trousers and a white corduroy shirt with a pocket. He carried his case with pencil sharpener, notebook and box of coloured pencils in a cloth sack. With his sisters sitting at other desks, he felt lonely and fearful.

His mother had always told him, ''You are going to grow up, go to school, study hard, so that you never need to be like your father.'' But Antonio, who loved his father so much, who loved his strength, his size, his beard, the way he walked along the roads, wanted nothing more than to be like him. He wanted this so much that he no longer took a bath in the nude when anyone else was there. When he dreamed that he was falling over a precipice and his mother said it was a sign of growing up, he was happy. He wanted to dream more and more so that he would be his father's size more quickly. And whenever he went somewhere with his father, he always measured the relative size of their shadows.

He kept this wish to himself, but it was no less strong. Without knowing what would happen at school, aside from learning how to read, write and do arithmetic in his head, Antonio was aware of a fear that made his whole body hurt.

Little by little Antonio's fears diminished. He had already begun gathering flowers from the path to decorate the teacher's desk. On leaving the classroom he would walk a ways along the road, up until the intersection, hand in hand with Miss Aurora. Her hand was gentle and soft and, even better, was able to make beautiful letters.

But the best part of school came at the end of the class. After they had copied their homework from the blackboard, Miss Aurora asked the pupils to put their things away. Then she would open a book and read another part of the story that talked of spring, summer, autumn and winter — enchanted stories where witches and fairies lived among kings and queens:

I don't know if I saw it, heard about it or lived through it. . . . the castle was all in gold and

surrounded by never-ending gardens of sunflow-
ers. The light pouring on the castle made it seem
as if the sun lived here on earth.

But there was no happiness in this castle. It
had been a long time since gaiety had passed
through the mirrored rooms or through the tow-
ers that reached up to touch the sky.

I don't know if I saw it, heard about it or lived
through it, but once upon a time, there was a
king, a queen and a princess who never smiled.
She had not smiled since the spring she was born.

That morning as the cold was beginning, the
antique wooden bowl, smooth and old, was full
of golden fried cakes covered with icing sugar
and cinnamon. They were called dreams, and
they smelled like a dream. When Mother told the
children that they would be drinking egg nog
instead of coffee that morning, their mouths
watered even more.

Seeing their joy, Mother had the sly look of
someone who was cheating someone else at a
game. She went around distributing the little
cakes and talking about the day, the cold, the
need to buy skin ointment and cocoa butter, the
work that was ahead of them, the lack of news
about their relatives. She tried not to look at the
children, who were unsuccessfully trying to chew

their cakes. The cakes were filled with cotton that she had put into a dream dough and then fried. The more the children pulled with their hands and teeth, the more she laughed. Suddenly, speaking in syllables, she said, "It's Ap-ril Fo-ool's Day!"

The children finally understood and began to take up the game, rolling up some of the cakes into white cloth to give as presents to their classmates. Mother prepared a plate with an ironed napkin as a present for the teacher.

Antonio was quiet all of a sudden. He bolted his mouth closed. His mother asked what the matter was, and said she was sorry. Nothing. He only spoke after a long time.

"I lost a tooth in the cotton."

"You'll get another one, that's the way it is," she said, smiling.

"Do you swear that it's not April Fool's Day for the tooth as well?"

"I swear. But to grow another you must throw your tooth behind you onto the roof."

"Oh, Mother. Is it the first of April all over again?"

And when their father arrived, warmly greeted by the children who were hoping to see him eat the cakes, he looked at Antonio a long time and moaned, "Did you leave the window open? Ah, you poor toothless thing!"

Antonio no longer filled whole pages with little balls to make an "a." He didn't have to think before writing that 1 was a stick, 2 a small duck, 3 a baby snake or 4 an upside-down chair. He was used to homework and would sing out his times tables high above the trees. "One times one is one, one times two is two . . ."

He was a devil in human form, people said. But the teacher praised him highly for his printing and his clean notebook, and for always having the answer on the tip of his tongue. Antonio always used to say sailboats even though he meant to say ships, but now he never confused the two. One day he learned that the order of factors does not alter the product.

Miss Aurora used a two-coloured pencil to correct the pupils' work. The pencil was blue on one side and red on the other. She would go from desk to desk inspecting, looking at nails, noticing buttons and the patches on uniforms. Nothing was prettier than having a notebook full of tens, sometimes in one colour, sometimes in the other.

Like the other children, Antonio wasn't concerned about knowing a lot. They all wanted to learn just to please the teacher.

The queen mother did everything to make the princess smile. She gave her stars, forests, pieces of the moon, birds' songs. One day the queen even let some butterflies in to dance in her daughter's dream. But she still did not smile.

On her birthday her mother gave her a sweet-singing hummingbird. The princess took the bird and gave it its freedom.

And the proud queen wept. She suffered so much that she began to fear that she would lose her own happiness.

The king was handsome. He had a long beard and an elegant and haughty walk. He dressed like a king: cape, crown and sceptre. He liked music, gardens, birds and woods. He loved his daughter as all fathers do and would have done anything to make her smile.

One day the father asked the angels to paint a rainbow in the sky for his daughter. She went off, as silent as peace, through the yellow of the rainbow. The birds held on to her hair. But the princess didn't smile.

Then the teacher would strike a bell that hung from the door, and the children would leave school sadly. The next day was too far away.

Antonio learned how to divide an apple into four, eight or even twelve parts in his head. He could talk about dozens, tens, hundreds and grosses.

One day the teacher told the class that an island was a piece of land surrounded by water on all sides. Antonio thought about his school and wondered what it should be called since it was surrounded by mountains on all sides. But the boy did not ask. He was never afraid of having doubts.

Antonio always arrived at school early. This way he was able to fill the water pot, sweep the classroom and clean the dust off the desks. It was important that everything be very clean to receive Miss Aurora's new ideas, he thought.

Sometimes, during a class of the agriculture club, the teacher would choose a bunch of lettuce or chicory and send it as a present to his mother. Maybe, who knows, to say thank you for the cakes of cotton!

After dictation, Miss Aurora would put exercises on the blackboard, in beautiful handwriting, for the most advanced pupils. Antonio would read them quickly, interested in knowing more about the three ships: *Santa Maria*, *Pinta* and *Niña*. He wasn't able to find out about the *Calmaria* that discovered Brazil with Pedro Alvares Cabral. But he knew that the sailboat had been decked out in white.

If the teacher talked about the solar system, the rotation of the earth, the proof that the earth was round, the east, west, north and south, he was all ears, paying close attention. He would forget his exercises, making long voyages beyond the horizon.

"All right children, see you Sunday, if God wishes, at the nine o'clock mass at the chapel. We have to prepare for your first communion."

A grownup child is double the work, Mother repeated, as she tucked Antonio's arm inside a tile close to his pillow so that he could sleep without being bothered too much by his broken arm.

He had climbed up on a bay horse bareback— no harness, nothing — holding on only by the mane. He fell. Luckily his father was at home and took the boy, white with pain and fear, to the city. The doctor secured his arm with bamboo stalks and tightly wound pieces of cloth. He gave him a prescription for pills to reduce the pain. Antonio went forty days without doing any work around the house. He had broken his right arm.

At first the pain was intense and didn't allow the boy to think of anything else. He would cry quietly the whole night long, with his arm lying on the tile cradle. When it got better, he returned to classes with his arm in a sling, carrying his reader in the other hand. As he was unable to write, he learned to remember things by heart just by listening.

They say that the fairies weave their spells during a full moon. Dressed in blue, they carry wands with a star at the end. And they make everything come true. There are no lies left in the world, Gofredo thought. He knew that it was the fairies who hid the rainbow inside each and every soap bubble. I would love to get to know a fairy, the boy dreamed.

And so it was. Gofredo left early for the forest to cut firewood. He was able to hear the sound of silence and talk with the birds. He knew how to tell the time by looking at the sky. But from that day on a new reality came to be.

Antonio was proceeding as slowly and carefully as if he were walking on a wire or stepping on eggs. His steps were sluggish. He couldn't stumble, fall or be startled. He knew that only his eye on the pen kept the ink from spilling. Without blinking, he would choose the path, controlling the series of events with footbridges and cattle-guards.

Miss Aurora had let them stop using a pencil. It was now time for pen and ink. Antonio had asked to borrow his father's ink well and pen, so his anxiety was doubled. He couldn't make a mistake because you couldn't wipe out ink with an eraser. You had to write correctly from the start.

Sometimes Antonio was so involved with the pen and ink that he forgot everything else. He began to dribble on the paper, messing up the whole page.

Anna cried a lot during the night. Her mother, walking with little cat steps, would get up and place small bits of pills, Dr. Lustosa wax and tooth medicine in the hole in the girl's tooth. Antonio imagined the taste of each remedy. He could even imagine the taste of the aloe juice that his mother put on her nipples to wean his sister. In fact he looked bitterly at the large clump of the plant in the yard.

Someone, I don't know if it was the godmother or not, came up with the idea of washing the girl's feet in lukewarm water and then having her use the water to gargle with. They tried every-thing. What is sure is that after a time the pains went away. Other teeth that were not milk teeth grew in.

Just as the rainy and dry seasons came back every year, so did the suffering, the losses and the fears.

The next day, during school, Antonio would be listless with sleep. He needed Miss Aurora to sing or wake him up with stories.

When the birds, as night was falling, wrote in the sky with their nocturnal feathers, Grandfather would read the signs of the winds, the colours and the clouds and foresee the coming of rain, harvest or cold.

Sometimes Father, listening to the weather, would read the silence and, freeing his tongue, translate its din into words from his childhood. Sometimes he would foretell the future written by God in wavy lines.

While she embroidered, Mother would read the arrival of letters, visitors and presents in the way the needle pricked her fingers and reddened the white linen. And when, between foam and soap powder, she rinsed the clothes in the corner of the water tank, the flight of insects would bring her foreshadowings of arrivals and departures, which she perceived in the beating of their wings.

"Ah," she would say, "I remember uncle's return after a long absence." Antonio would look into her eyes slowly and understand that he could lie in her lap and sob, and thereby relieve his great sadness.

In school, the teacher was teaching the pupils how to read. Antonio learned without effort. He already knew that you could learn a lot more from reading between the letters and their silences. It was possible to travel into distant worlds, worlds that the eye could not see, but a book could bring. And from that point on, only a pencil was needed for Antonio to begin to write.

The End of the Day

A NTONIO began to swallow everything whole, without chewing. He looked as if he had the mumps all over again, because he was all swollen. But he was in training for his first communion.

"If the host touches a tooth, the taste of blood comes immediately," they said. And his fear of biting God grew.

There was always something to be afraid of. With every day, the more his terror intensified, the more he swallowed everything whole, without chewing it, right to the bottom of his throat. He thought of not going to the communion, of having a stomach ache, or putting garlic under his arm to get a fever, but all this would be committing yet another sin.

Ready on top of the crystal cabinet was a white candle wrapped with ribbon and with a P and a X drawn on it—the marks for Christ and peace. Antonio's mother had made him a suit with a white shirt and bow tie, while she was thinking about what snacks to prepare for the morning coffee.

But fear continued to grow in the boy's heart. At times he thought that it was the temptation of the devil, and he couldn't bear to be alone any-where in the house. He was afraid of his own shadow. Even in the bathtub he would have the Ten Commandments at his fingertips:

> Love God above all
> Don't take His name in vain . . .
> Don't covet your neighbour's things
> Honour your father and mother.

Sometimes he thought of praying to Our Lady, but in religion class the teacher had explained that Our Lady was a woman so beautiful that it was impossible to imagine her. And praying to someone that you couldn't envision was even more difficult.

But the day arrived. Antonio, fasting, was with his fellow students in the first row of the chapel awaiting the moment and anxiously drying his mouth. He received the host. It clung to the roof of his mouth and slowly melted.

The photographer was waiting at the exit. They had put up a very large painting on the wall of the church, showing Christ holding a chalice and the host. Each child kneeled in genuflection as the photographer, standing behind a black cloth, took the photo. It was a trick—each child receiving communion from the hands of God.

Antonio's parents framed the photo and hung it close to the guardian angel in his bedroom. It was his first certificate.

In school, Antonio learned that Pedro Alvares Cabral discovered Brazil in 1500. He learned that the sun was a star of the fifth magnitude, that one gross was equal to 144, and that a league was six kilometres. He knew how to recite the ''Highway Cross,'' was overcome with pity for the slaves in the hold of the slave ships who had died of melancholy, and he could sing a song to make the seeds stay nice and warm on Tree Day. He drew maps of Brazil's regions on cardboard, using a sharp coloured pencil and later perforating everything with a needle to create relief to indicate the mountains.

He got to know other children in school. They would meet on the weekends to go fishing, swim in the streams, walk in the bush, talk about their girlfriends and smoke cigarettes made of dried chayote stalks, which burned their throats. Sometimes they caught frogs and put cigarettes in their mouths until they burst. And when the marches of the ants took place, they would wait for the scorpions to appear and then encircle them with hot coals and watch them commit suicide.

June 12 was St. Antonio's day, patron saint of the chapel. There was always a mass and a procession, a band and bonfires. That year Antonio's father was in charge. Days ahead, his mother put flowers made of bread dough on the branches of a maidenhair fern to decorate the wooden framework that carried the statue in the procession. The girls dressed as angels, and Mother and Father were at the front of the procession holding the pole wrapped in crêpe paper. Strong Jose carried the framework with the statue. Antonio was the only one with nothing to do.

I don't know whose idea it was, but Antonio and his schoolmates filled their pockets with lemons. When the band began to play, they sucked the lemons in front of the musicians. Everything went out of tune. The musicians were unable to play because of the pain that they felt at the base of their ears.

At lunchtime there was baked rice, sausages and beans, hardboiled eggs, baked chicken, pork, macaroni, steamed rice and cassava. In front of the priest, Antonio's father told his son that he had made him sad. After that the boy never wanted to eat lemons again.

Time didn't leave Antonio behind. After having witnessed many departures, it was his turn. A few days before, his mother spent time organizing his clothes. She made small repairs, adjusted buttons, reinforced the hems of his pants—which were long now — and darned his socks. Then, with a fine thread, she embroidered the letter ''A'' on each piece of his clothing. As she worked, she would say things like, "You must not stop sending word. You always have a messenger. Even just a short note will do." "I will send you sweets from time to time." "Your grandfather will be happy. He's so alone in that big house."

His father, to break the boy's silence, played at arithmetic with him, recited the times tables, listed the capitals of Brazil and asked Antonio to respond with the respective states.

On the last day of class, the teacher, with the same affection as on the first day, told him, "This is as much as I can teach. The rest has to be done at another school. Don't be afraid. Pay attention. Study the things that you know least about. Do everything without hurrying. Think before you act. I will miss you, but Anna will be here with me and I know that she will bring me news of you."

Antonio couldn't sleep that night. He sensed the smell of the lights being put out, the cheeps of lost birds, the rooster waking at dawn. Rolled up in his bed, he wished he could disappear slowly, so as not to cause any grief.

Antonio left with his father in the truck. He kissed his mother's hand and embraced his siblings without saying a word. He was suffering. It was a pain that only crying could cure, but he didn't want to cry and force the others to grieve with him.

They drove along the road in silence. Once in a while his father looked at him out of the corner of his eye without saying anything. Everything was being left behind: the cattle, the streams, the bridges, the fields, the trees. The truck ate up the road, covering Antonio's face with dust so that he could not see the way back home. There was a heavy silence, as if he were already feeling homesick for everything he was leaving behind. And with each turn the unknown seemed both closer and farther away.

They arrived at his grandfather's house. Antonio got down, asked for his grandfather's blessing and didn't bother to go into the kitchen. He knew that it had been a long time since his grandmother was alive. He went up to his big bedroom and left his suitcase on the bed at the back of the room. The rest of the room was full of emptiness.

His father did not want to travel at night and so wanted to leave quickly. They held each other closely. His father's eyes moistened. He looked at his son and said, ''I think I've caught a cold.''

''Me, too,'' the boy responded, understanding.

I don't know how many years have passed. I do know that I'm always getting word of Antonio: in bowls of rice pudding in highway restaurants, in the water that falls from the church bell on rainy days, in boxes of coloured pencils in shop windows, in the smell of baked rice, in the block of sun coming through a window, in the roots of jaboticabas, in the rainbow and the "widow's wedding," in aquariums full of fish, in children crossing the streets in uniform, in a fried egg on rice, in news of premature births, in the rounds of salami in supermarkets, in fairy stories, in the devil's birds flying in churches, in rattlesnakes, bands, lemons, horseshoes and goat's milk, in apples without purple paper, in branches of fennel, pennyroyal and anise, in the rainy season, in the dry season, in the cicadas singing at the end of the afternoon, in runny noses and whooping cough, in the smell of corrals, in paths and shortcuts, in cocoa butter on cold nights, in pictures of the sea, in the taste of tears, in chickens and their nests, in bonfires on St. Antonio's day and Palm Sundays, in the fear of devils and ghosts on birthdays, in the bees' visits to the flowers, in the smell of egg nog, in the first star that I see at night, in the cheese melted on slices of cake, in wooden school cases, in pencilled messages, in fruits out of season, in white notebooks, in conversations and silences, in departures and arrivals.

There is no way to forget him. Even when I'm trying to pay attention to my work, if I should happen to start writing with a red or blue pen, or if an ant or the shadow of a bird in flight goes by, if I see clouds or lightning, if I go into a chapel or walk through a park, Antonio doesn't leave me. And I don't know which of us has more fear or more love.

Other International Fiction Contest winners

Norway

Kissing in the Wind *by* Rune Belsvik
Translated and adapted by Torild Homstad *and*
  Shelley Tanaka

On a tiny windswept island off the coast of Norway, the members of the Windholm Brass Band are desperately trying to think of a way to raise money for new uniforms. Can the people of Windholm really stand yet another bake sale or Bingo night? And if the band doesn't come up with the money for new uniforms, will the ruthless sea winds simply sweep their faded and tattered jackets right off their bodies, forcing them to march stark naked?

Then the band's treasurer hears that the famous American actress, Krystall Evenes, is searching for her Scandinavian roots, and gradually a brilliant scheme is born.

ISBN 0-88899-087-1
$9.95

Denmark

Mondays Will Never Be the Same
  by Martin Elmer
Translated by Kenneth Tindall *and* Shelley Tanaka

Daniel Rehsel is 14½ years old—too young, in his opinion, to be burdened with so many problems. His single father refuses to look for a suitable second wife, his grandparents are constantly embarrassing him, his crush on a beautiful 22-year-old Susanne is going nowhere, and his teacher is a racist who seems to hold a particular grudge against Daniel. Not only that, but the school show is coming up, and Daniel's brilliant monologue is being ruthlessly rewritten by a couple of girls!

Can things get any worse? It appears so, when Moses, a bum, is found sleeping in the Rehsels' basement, and Moses's "daughter" turns out to be a transvestite who is interested in Daniel's father!

ISBN 0-88899-072-3
$8.95

Sweden

Camel Bells *by* Janne Carlsson
Translated by Angela Barnett-Lindberg

Imagine waking up one morning to find a foreign army taking over your country . . .

This is what happens to twelve-year-old Hajdar who, after his father's death, suddenly finds himself the head of his family. In his new role the boy must make many adult decisions. After the Russians invade his homeland of Afghanistan, he is faced with the toughest choice of all when he must decide whether or not to run away from his own country.

ISBN 0-88899-080-4
$8.95

Canada

False Face *by* Welwyn Wilton Katz

One day Laney McIntyre and Tom Walsh discover two old Indian masks in a nearby bog. The leering, grimacing faces are terrifying, but even more horrible is what lies beneath them.

As the mystery surrounding the masks unfolds, Laney and Tom must come to grips with the real and terrible power of the masks themselves, and the danger they pose to those who try to control them.

"Steeped in Indian mythology and modern-day family drama, *False Face* is terrifying and exciting." Maclean's

"Katz has produced a sure-fire thriller . . . " Montreal Gazette

ISBN 0-88899-082-0
$7.95